The Gorgon and the Stranger

The Bright One Series

Ashley L. Castillo

Published by Ashley L. Castillo, 2021.

This is a work of fiction. Similarities to real people, places, or events are entirely coincidental.

THE GORGON AND THE STRANGER

First edition. April 30, 2021.

Copyright © 2021 Ashley L. Castillo.

ISBN: 979-8215261484

Written by Ashley L. Castillo.

Dedication

This short story is dedicated to all the people who make friendship mean something. It's not every day you can connect with someone who changes your life forever.

Here's to the friendships that never change over time, the friends that you can go months without talking to and pick up right where you left off, the friends that you talk to every day, and the ones that make your life brighter just by being in it!

This is for you, with all my love...

The Gorgon and the Stranger

Blood, screams, chaos.

The world around Euryale disappeared as a prophetic vision took hold. It was the kind of vision that left her terrified and disoriented after. She saw her sisters' faces smeared with blood. Their bodies twisted and broken. Medusa's beautiful form had been ravaged, and Stheno…it was too gruesome to put into words what had been left of her.

Euryale blinked in the cave's familiar surroundings, where she and her sisters hid, secluded from the rest of the realm. The snakes that were part of her dangled around her face, moving and weaving against her skull, and her shoulders pressed in close for comfort.

Her snakes couldn't speak, but they didn't need to. It was as if their tiny minds and hers were connected. She was them, and they were her. They moved and functioned on their own, and yet they were of one mind.

The prophecies took hold often enough that Euryale had no fear of them, yet what she usually saw within the visions made her tremble. She'd seen her sisters in this one, but someone else too. Perhaps the one who would bring on this vision, who would hurt her sisters so?

The visions weren't always clear, and this one was vague enough that Euryale wasn't sure quite when it would happen. The sharper the visions became, and the more detailed they were, the sooner they'd come to be. This one was fuzzy around the edges. There was still time to change the fate of this path.

Euryale stroked her snakes with soft reassurance. But it wasn't a moment later when her youngest sister slithered into the cavern, a look of pure fear on her gorgeous face.

"A man, a stranger, has entered our territory," Medusa said, her voice quivering with fear.

The prophecy Euryale had just had sank into her stomach, making her see red. She'd do anything it took to protect her sisters.

"Did he touch you?" she asked her sister instantly.

"No." Medusa shook her head, sending her snakes hissing. "If he had, he'd be stone. Still, he feels powerful."

That one word, powerful, was enough to send a warning tingle through Euryale's spine down to the tip of her tail. Someone powerful enough to kill her and her sisters? Could this be the other person in her vision? Or was it just a coincidence?

The inhabitants of the Land of the Beasts usually knew to steer clear of the Gorgons' territory. Medusa left the stone statues of her latest kills to deter them.

Still, other clan members would come seeking them out from time to time, looking for trouble. Others, desperate for food, would come sniffing around too. But all the Beasts and Creatures of the realm knew; they entered Gorgon territory at their own risk.

Clearly, this stranger didn't think them a threat. Euryale was about to teach him how very wrong he was.

"Tell Stheno when she returns that I went hunting."

Medusa gulped and nodded. "Be careful. The stranger entered near the gorge. There are many places to hide nearby."

Euryale gave her sister a reassuring smile. She and her sisters enjoyed springing on unsuspecting prey there for just that reason.

"You too. Make sure you and Stheno stay inside the cavern until I return. I had a prophecy take hold not long ago."

Her sister looked uneasy but knew enough not to ask more questions if Euryale didn't outright tell her.

"I'll be back soon."

~

Euryale crouched in the underbrush, watching the stranger as he danced through the trees. A strange one, this man.

The trespasser turned, climbing effortlessly up several hard rocks, headed north. Neither she nor her snakes could tell what he was.

Strange—a scent she didn't know or recognize. Dangerous, most likely; clearly fit, judging from how he quickly moved up the rocks.

She'd been trailing him for the past hour or so. He traveled alone. At least there was that. But he didn't seem to be going anywhere in particular.

From the distance she kept, he was simply a moving body. No distinct features could be seen, just a blur of black clothing and a billowing cloak trailing behind him.

All the same, Euryale watched as he'd pause, looking up at the trees and turning from time to time. Once she thought she saw him shrug and then turn a different direction almost immediately after.

She wondered where he was going. Why was he in her lands? What was he up to? She'd find out soon. It was almost sunset.

She'd gone to the place where Medusa said she'd spotted him. Euryale had checked the gorge and all its usual hiding places until she found his trail. It was difficult for her to pick up. He was smart this one, probably used to traveling alone and covering his steps.

But these were her woods, and no matter how carefully he trod, how few twigs he snapped, how he seemed to jump from rock to rock and not disturb a thing, she could see his trail and followed.

She couldn't see a gleam of weapons upon the stranger but knew that meant nothing. He probably had one hidden under his cloak. Euryale was waiting for nightfall so she could kill him. But she had to be cautious. She and her sisters knew all too well how quickly hunters could become the hunted.

And this one was clever. Euryale could tell that already. Odd though he might seem, without purpose and direction, she could tell he was up to something. But what it was, she couldn't begin to guess.

She didn't follow the trespasser directly as he moved. She never touched a single place on the soil or rocks that he had. Instead, Euryale circled, keeping a wide berth between herself and the path he'd carved through her land.

He was going up and up, and she knew why. From on high, he could keep an eye out for predators like her. In the darkness of the nights, nothing was safe within the Land of the Beasts. Hunters came out, all kinds. While there were none in this part of the forest, the stranger probably didn't know that, not if he didn't realize this was her territory.

She and her sisters let nothing, not Beast or Creature or anything in between, dwell in their lands. They had carved out a large area that this stranger would be right in the middle of come nightfall.

She circled slowly, climbing up the side of the incline as the stranger reached the top. He turned and looked back. Euryale stilled, even knowing he'd never be able to spot her.

She was right. A moment later, after a glance over his shoulder, the stranger slipped out of sight, going behind a large boulder at the top of the hill. It was where he'd sleep tonight, thinking it an advantageous spot, but it would be the death of him.

~

Euryale slithered slowly, wrapping her way this way and that through the trees until she'd moved to the opposite side of the hill. She could see the trespasser, but only just.

He was well hidden in the shadows of the large rock on high. With his dark clothing wrapped around him, it was almost impossible to detect him. But she did. She knew every rock and tree and shadow within her domain, and this one did not belong.

The sun was setting behind him, and still, the trespasser made no move to light a fire. That gave her pause. The ones that made fires were easy to kill, easy to sneak up on, using the light and darkness to her advantage. If this one didn't have a fire and was using the light of the stars to see by, he might spot her before she could snap his neck.

She watched him and waited as the sun's last weak rays disappeared and the stars came out. He didn't move much. Occasionally his head would tilt this way or that. Once he stretched out a foot, flexed it, and brought it back in.

For a while, he stopped moving altogether, and she thought he must be sleeping. If she weren't so cautious, she would've slithered forward and been done with it. But she didn't.

Caution had kept her and her sisters alive, but it was tempered with a fear that she always tried to push back. Once in a while, it would creep in on her. Tonight, sitting watching the stranger, Euryale felt it trickling in at the back of her mind. She shoved it away.

It didn't matter how many of them she and her sisters killed. It didn't matter how much blood was spilled or how many turned to stone. When it was done, her hands would shake, and she'd fall into herself and the memories of her past life like a boulder rolling off a cliff, fast and with nothing to stop it until it slammed into the ground and shattered.

Once she was broken all over again, the death and blood a constant reminder, she'd sleep. The next day she'd pretend she was whole again, as her sisters did. They did it to survive. They had no choice.

The stranger hadn't moved for a long time. It was deep in the night. It was time to kill him and return home. She and her sisters all had different killing methods. Hers was very physical.

Euryale liked to make her kills as personal as possible, in contrast to Medusa, who killed from afar with a single gaze. Stheno was somewhere in between. She usually slit her victim's throats, or if she was feeling lazy, used her various traps in the woods.

It was a shame this one hadn't accidentally found one of those and saved her the effort.

Euryale slithered forward, keeping to the shadows and trees. Her snakes were silent and still. Everything was quiet in the forest.

When she and her sisters had first been cursed, they hadn't known how to use their new bodies, but that had been long ago. That had been in a different age, when all the species of the world had dwelled together before the Great War. Now Euryale no longer recalled what it had been like to have legs or what color her hair had been before her snakes had replaced it.

Her serpentine body moved to her will as if it had always been hers, as it would always be hers. She twisted around the boulder, coming up from behind the sleeping stranger.

Her snakes tasted the air. All seemed fine. Euryale lifted herself with her tail to perch on top of the boulder, sitting on the back end. The stranger was huddled in the shadows just beneath her. His life would be over soon, and then she could get back to hers, knowing the vision she'd seen earlier would never come to pass.

Her tail stretched and wrapped around the boulder. Euryale was concentrated on the shadow below her, not on what her tail was doing. She was watching him for any sign of movement or that he detected her. Her tail slithered silently toward his wrist that was lying on the ground. Wrist, ankle, neck; it didn't matter what body part it was. She just needed something to grab, and then it would be over.

Her tail was right about to touch him when he spoke in a strange gravelly tone.

"Don't."

She stopped moving. Stopped breathing. Her snakes quivered by her neck. How she hated men and their voices. How she hated and feared them.

"You've been following me for hours," he said slowly.

Still, he didn't move, and she didn't dare to. If he'd known that she was there, then he'd been planning this.

A trap. But how would it spring?

"I just needed to rest for a few hours. Then I'll be on my way. I suggest you do the same."

The audacity of his words brought back her hatred in full. Who did he think he was? This was her part of the forest, where she and her sisters ruled.

THE GORGON AND THE STRANGER

Who was this man to say he could come and go? And of all things to tell her to go? As if he was doing her a favor.

Never.

She would die first.

Her tail lashed out, grabbing his wrist. It took seconds to slam him into the rock he'd been hiding under and wrap her body around his, squeezing.

She pushed his chest back, and his hood fell from his face. A strange one this Creature in her grasp was; she'd never seen the likes of him before. His luminescent green eyes glared at her.

"Don't," he growled as she squeezed.

Her hand pressed hard to his chest. His arms and legs were bound in her coils. He was helpless, and she'd make him beg for his life, squeezing him inch by inch to make his death as painful as all the memories that she and her sisters had suffered. And only when he screamed as she'd screamed, only when he cried and wished for death as she had would she kill him.

"I don't want to hurt you," he grunted as she tightened her grip.

Euryale pressed her hand harder to his chest. His heartbeat was strong. His skin was warm beneath his clothes. But soon, it would be as cold as she was.

She squeezed again, harder. She was tired of his words. She wanted to make him scream. She heard the crunch as her coils tightened. And yet the stranger did nothing.

He didn't make a sound. He didn't seem to notice that she'd just broken several bones. His face looked empty, and she wondered if she'd accidentally snapped his spine and killed him before she could have her fun.

"I didn't want to do this," he hissed.

Then he transformed. She was thrown back, slamming hard into the trees that she'd hidden in. He let loose a roar that sent a wash of cold dread down her body.

Fear and pain mingled together into a hazy potion of confusion so thick she was choking on it. The stranger was on her in a moment, right in her face as she sagged against the tree.

He'd kill her.

Come the dawn when her sisters came looking for her, they'd find nothing but her bones.

She'd had no idea what he was by his smell and form. He certainly hadn't looked enough like his transformed state to give her warning.

But there was no denying what he was now as he loomed over her. Euryale couldn't believe her eyes. She hadn't known there were any—

"You're going to have a headache when you wake up," the trespasser snarled, and then Euryale's head snapped back, and everything went dark.

~

"Euryale?" It was Medusa's sweet, tentative voice that called to her.

A familiar hand touched her face, and she opened her eyes. Her sisters were staring down at her, equal parts worry and relief on their faces.

"I told you she'd be fine," the male voice said, bringing a hiss to Euryale's lips as she turned to follow the sound.

Something about this wasn't right, Euryale realized through pain searing along her skull and neck. This couldn't be real.

The trespasser was still alive and in their cavern. He was standing on the far side of the room, looking amused. He would've never been allowed to live upon meeting her sisters. They would've killed him.

And if he'd been the one she thought responsible for her vision, she and her sisters would be dead already.

This must be a hallucination of sorts. Could he do magic? Was he inside her mind? She'd heard of such dark powers before. That could be the only explanation.

All the same, even if he wasn't a threat to them now, he could be later. This Creature, whatever he might be, couldn't be allowed to live.

She lurched up, ready to attack him. Stheno slammed her palm into her chest, knocking Euryale back into the bed with a grunt of pain. Her oldest sister had always been relatively strong, but the pain blooming in her chest made her wonder how much of this was real.

"Be still, sister," Medusa said, stroking her with gentle fingers. "We already tried to kill him several times."

She blinked, not understanding. Euryale looked at her sisters' faces, trying to read them, and for once couldn't. Too many emotions were coursing within all of them for one to make itself known. Even her snakes seemed confused as they writhed around her shoulders, moving, tasting, not understanding.

Her eyes traveled back to the stranger, who had a slight smile tugging the corner of his lips up as she looked at him.

How dare he think any of this was funny? Euryale glared at him.

"The one stared at me until she started to cry," he explained in his rough tones as he played with a bloody cloth in his hands. "And the other one attempted to slit my throat. She got me pretty good, but not good enough."

She didn't like his implications at all. Euryale didn't like that he was in their cavern. She didn't like any of this. She felt helpless and afraid all over again.

She tried to sit up, but again her sisters quickly pushed her back into the bed, fussing over her and telling her about her head injury. The injury this bastard had given her.

"Get out," she snarled.

The stranger nodded. "That was my plan. I wanted to make sure you woke up first and that the three of you don't attempt to mess with me again. As I tried to tell you, I was just passing through. On the other side of that rock formation, as I'm sure you know, is a stream. That's my destination. I would've slipped into it and been out of your territory well before dawn if you'd listened to me."

She didn't know what to make of his words. Why would he care if she woke? If his destination had been so close, then why hadn't he just kept going? If that were true, he could've slipped into the stream and lost her and saved them both a lot of trouble.

Oh, she would've been furious to lose her prey, but even that would've been preferable to waking and finding him in her cave with her sisters.

"You have our permission to pass. But do so swiftly," Stheno said stiffly.

Euryale couldn't believe her ears. How could her sisters just think to let him go after all he'd done? If he lived and told others about them and their weakness, it would be as good as dying now.

She was about to protest when Medusa's snakes began hissing a low warning. Her snakes understood. They'd form a plan once he was gone.

The trespasser was watching them cautiously as they watched him. They might be on opposite sides of the room and might've been speaking civilly, but there was no trust between them. Her sisters surrounding her were as stiff-backed as he was. His posture spoke volumes, as if he was ready to fight his way out.

Euryale tilted her head toward the door. The stranger nodded, pulling a black bag she hadn't noticed higher up his shoulder. He turned his back to them as he turned to exit. It made her cold blood start to boil. The insult in that alone was reason enough to fight him all over again.

She and her sisters watched as the tall, strangely graceful Creature exited from their cavern and slipped into the trees.

"What's the plan to kill him?" she asked her sisters instantly.

It was Medusa who sighed and shook her head.

"There isn't one. I tried to turn him to stone. You should've seen how stupid I looked standing there glaring at him as he dropped your body on the ground between us."

"Was he in this form?" Euryale asked, wondering if the Creature she'd seen after she slammed into the trees had been real.

"Yes. But whatever he is, he isn't Human enough for my stone to take hold of him. And Stheno's blade and skills were no match for him."

Euryale's snakes hissed when she did. This was unacceptable.

"We can't let him live. If he does, he'll tell others, and they'll come for us again."

"We don't have a choice," Stheno said sadly. "We don't stand a chance against him."

"We can die trying to kill him or die when they come hunting us again. Which would you prefer?" Euryale snapped angrily at her sisters. She hated this situation. There was no way out, and her head was pounding.

"We can move," Medusa said softly. "We can run to another cavern and hide."

Euryale snarled and slammed her fist into the hard ground where they slept. They'd hidden away for years. They'd run before, and every time it never did them any good.

"I don't want to keep running. We've built a reputation—a good one. The other Beasts are cautious of us now. If we run, we undo everything. If we run, we become those weak girls again. If we run, it's as good as letting them kill us. It's my fault that the threat is still alive. I'll take care of this, and if I can't, then I'll die trying," she told her sisters.

Stheno let out a long slow breath. She'd probably known it would come to this. Medusa looked like she was going to cry. Euryale's younger, more beautiful sister knew all too well about guilt regarding who was responsible for their situation. After all, it had been Medusa who'd doomed them all to this fate.

"Do you want us to come?" was all her little sister could manage before the tears rolled down her face.

They knew the answer. It was the same as it would always be, as it ever was. Euryale would try to protect them.

"I'll go alone. And this time, that monster won't stand a chance."

~

She and her sisters had always dwelled in the part of the forest where the Land of the Beasts was. It had always just been the three of them, surviving together. She never recalled anyone protecting them. They'd always had to fend for themselves, three girls, skinny, malnourished, and practically feral, living the best way they'd known how.

There had been a village nearby. They'd gotten stones thrown at them, and harsh words yelled in all the tongues of the world, telling them they were unwanted.

Still, some part of them, that Human part perhaps, had always wanted to be near others. They'd slink to the town's edges, cross its paths in the dead of night, looking for scraps.

Then things had begun to change when their bodies did—shifting from young girls to young women.

Hunters often went out from the village, and the girls had always been wary and hid from the weapons, having learned long ago what pain they brought. Still, the girls were as curious about others as they were cautious.

It had only been a matter of time before they crossed paths with a man. He'd gotten separated from his hunting party. They'd been hiding nearby. Fear had made them immobile as he approached. They knew better than to run, for when you ran in the forest, predators gave chase.

He'd blinked at them, stunned for a moment, and then did the oddest thing another Human had ever done. He'd smiled at them instead of snarling.

He'd asked what they were doing alone in the woods. He'd asked if he could help them.

Euryale hadn't trusted him. The other Humans had never been kind to them. But he'd spoken so sweetly, as if the thought of hurting them would've never crossed his mind. They'd wanted so badly to believe that lie, to belong.

Medusa had smiled back and, before either Euryale or Stheno could think to stop her, she told the man they dwelled nearby in the woods. That they didn't need help but that they were always cautious when hunting parties went by.

Euryale didn't recall precisely how the interaction had ended, but they'd stayed in their hiding place while the man moved off.

After that, Medusa had been drawn to Humans like a moth to a flame. Her youngest sister was constantly watching the hunting parties, getting purposely close.

The man they'd met came hunting time and time again. And Euryale would watch as he'd slow and turn off the path, searching the trees and underbrush for them.

He'd been middle-aged, with kind eyes. He'd started bringing them food from the village or leaving a portion of his kill behind if he didn't. Medusa begged to be allowed to speak with him again, but Euryale and Stheno had forbidden her. They'd known just because one Human was kind didn't mean they all were. Years of harsh treatment couldn't be made up for by one.

Euryale hadn't had her prophetic powers then. She hadn't known something was wrong, exactly, but she'd known right away one morning that something was different. Medusa had returned all smiles back to their hidden home. When Euryale and Stheno had asked what had made their sister so happy, Medusa just shrugged.

But then this started to occur every day, Medusa leaving alone before Euryale or Stheno woke. They usually went in pairs at the least, though sometimes they went alone.

But it was Medusa's insistence at going alone time and time again that finally made Euryale and Stheno follow her one day.

They trailed her for several hours before arriving near a large flat river. Curious what their sister was doing, they stayed in the shadows.

Nothing seemed wrong except this place was far from where they usually hunted. Being this far from their familiar territory was dangerous.

Medusa had gone to the riverbed, stripping out of the ragged clothes they'd stolen and dipping into the water. It was nothing unusual for them to bathe. Still, why go far from home?

Euryale's breath hitched when a face surfaced from within the river. It was hard to miss him, with red hair like liquid fire. Handsome he was, but the gills on his neck as he watched her sister from the rocks marked him as a Mer.

She'd heard stories about the Merpeople drowning unsuspecting swimmers. Euryale hadn't thought about it. She'd instantly moved from her hiding place, shouting at Medusa to get out of the water, asking her what she'd been doing so far from home.

The Mer behind the rocks didn't slink away as she'd been expecting. And to her horror, her sister had turned, looking over her shoulder at him, and waded out of the water almost reluctantly.

When they'd gotten home, Euryale and Stheno had been furious. Medusa had shrugged it off, evading their questions. After that, they kept a closer eye on her, but their sister would manage to slink away from time to time, in the dead of night.

It had been sometime later, several months perhaps, that Euryale and Stheno had woken and found Medusa gone again. They'd searched everywhere for her, going so far as to split up and look as far as the river. But they found no sign of her.

By the time the entire day had passed and night had set in once more, and Medusa still hadn't returned, they were frightened and worried beyond imagining.

Three days their sister had been gone before Stheno made the unthinkable suggestion that they should try the village and see if anyone might talk to them. If someone might have seen Medusa.

It was pure desperation that drove them to it. Together Euryale and Stheno had gone, cautiously entering the town that they had crept through for years, entering the place they knew was common for the villagers to meet at.

The stares they'd received were something Euryale had never forgotten, even after all this time. The villagers had seemed shocked to see them, hostile, and a little mesmerized at the same time.

Cautiously, they'd approached a man who looked similar to the kind one who'd fed them. They'd asked him and the others around his table if they'd seen Medusa.

"Oh, the pretty one?" the man had asked. But before Euryale could answer, he continued, "She comes around here all the time. She took off with Perseus yesterday. Haven't seen them since though."

Euryale remembered feeling shocked at the casualness of this statement. But somehow she'd managed to ask if the man knew where they'd gone.

"Out by the lake most likely; it's good hunting on the way and not bad fishing either. A bunch of the boys kept talking about building up that way."

She and Stheno hadn't known where this lake was. But the man had given them good enough directions that she thought they could find it. They'd set off with their hearts in their throats, wondering what danger their little sister had brought upon them.

Euryale could never have guessed.

They'd found the lake. They'd found their sister in a man's arms, smiling and touching and laughing. How happy she had looked, naked by the edge of the water.

They'd ruined the happy look on her face. They'd yelled at her, told her how terrified they'd been. They told her to come home.

The man, Perseus, had stood between them and their sister as if he was protecting her from them instead of the other way around. When they'd told Medusa to come, she'd refused. And Perseus had told them they were in love and that he planned to marry her.

Euryale had been reeling from the news, shocked and disbelieving, not understanding. Stheno had been furious and had tried to grab their sister to shake some sense into her. But the man had shoved her away. Euryale remembered the shocked silence that had fallen on them as Stheno had hit the ground with a painful yelp.

Medusa had come around then, apologizing, but the man had stayed standing as he was, fists curled, ready to fight them if they took their sister away.

Euryale had begged, and Stheno, still angry and now humiliated with pain, tried her best to convince Medusa. But she refused, shaking her head, looking up at the man with such love in her eyes.

They wouldn't abandon her. When she refused to come, they finally decided that they would stay.

Medusa had told them Perseus had chosen the spot by the lake to build a home for them and that several of the men from the village were going to do the same. If the sisters all stayed together, they could be part of this new village where they'd belong.

It had seemed too good to be true.

Weeks passed in this strange new life. Euryale and Stheno still felt like outsiders, but now, they felt like outsiders to their sister and her new life. Medusa never left Perseus' side. She slept with him, ate with him, talked with him. Every breath she drew was for him.

Other men had come from the village. Euryale had felt out of place and unwelcome, where Medusa would smile at every man and laugh at every joke as if they'd never been the ones to throw stones at them before.

Perhaps they hadn't, these men. They were young and strapping, probably children when the sisters were. But still, even the other children of the village had never befriended or defended them when they'd been younger. Medusa, it seemed, had forgotten.

But Euryale hadn't, so when the men approached her, making advances, she'd turn them away. One went so far as to try to grab her, and she struck him in the face to get away and made sure always to be as near to Stheno and Medusa as she could get after that.

One morning, Euryale woke to the sounds of Medusa screaming. She and Stheno went running, as many of the others around them had. But the sight they saw couldn't prepare them for what came next.

A woman dripping in water, with gray hair and salt-stained clothes, stood towering above Medusa. Their sister's arm was hard in her grip. Medusa was naked from bathing, hair dripping, screeching in agony as the woman, with hatred etched on her face, twisted her arm harder.

No one moved but Euryale and Stheno. None of the men, not even Medusa's precious Perseus, lifted a finger to help her.

Euryale shoved the woman hard while Stheno tried to pull Medusa away. But the woman struck, landing a blow to Euryale's face that left her reeling, hot blood spilling from her nose.

"You dare to lay your filthy hands upon the Goddess of Water?" the woman roared.

Euryale had heard of the Goddess, of course. But she'd never seen her. She hadn't known.

"Do you know what this girl who you are trying to defend has done?"

Medusa was crying. Everything was a blur of pain. Euryale didn't understand why no one was saying anything, why no one was helping them.

"She chose a mortal over my son. She spurned him, heedless of the repercussions of her actions. And then this lust-filled snake had the audacity to bathe in my waters, to live by a lake after the destruction that she caused."

"No," Medusa had whispered. "I never—"

But Medusa never got the words out.

"For her crimes and yours for aiding her, I lay a curse upon you."

The Goddess' voice thundered as she grew to her godly size, until all Euryale could smell was the tang of salt, and all she could feel was pain as her body split apart, twisting and reshaping into something monstrous.

~

The pain of her transformation had been unbearable. While they lay in the mud, thrashing and writhing, everything had appeared in flashes, in bits of sounds.

The screams had changed. There was grunting and the sounds of skin slamming into skin; her sisters crying.

Euryale hadn't understood the sounds through the pain. She hadn't understood until the man whom she'd slapped swam into her vision. Pain was already searing along her body. Yet when his heavy weight and stinking breath settled on her, there was a whole other kind of pain she'd never imagined. She clawed, trying to fight. But one of the others grabbed her hands.

She could hear her sisters, and she fought to try to reach them, to try to help, but there were too many men.

By the time the men had finished with them, Euryale and her sisters lay half dead in the mud by the lake. So many man smells were upon her skin that she felt sick to her stomach, but she was afraid to touch the water to rinse off.

She heard her sisters weeping. They were alive. They'd survived, but their new bodies were hideous. They were bruised and bloody, weak and reeling.

Euryale remembered clawing her way toward them and then passing out from the effort.

When she came to, it was to the sound of a voice she didn't recognize. It was night, the stars shining bright above, and the small, hunched Creature that walked oddly came into focus. One sharp eye peered down at her in the darkness.

It was an old crone, an ugly woman. But that was what Euryale and her sisters were now too; ugly and monstrous.

"I usually keep to the woods too. It is safer there," the woman told her, reaching out tentatively toward Euryale's face. She was too tired to flinch, too tired to fight.

"I saw what happened, the truth of it all. I saw what you tried to do for the sake of your sister."

Euryale felt tears spring to her eyes. She'd tried to help, was all. She'd tried to keep Medusa safe, but in the end, she'd failed. She'd been weak and helpless to stop any of it.

"Your sister was foolish to think she could play with the hearts of males. And you were foolish to think you could make any difference to the cruelties that run rampant in the world."

Something loud snapped within the trees nearby, and a hunter's howl went piercing into the night.

"I must return to my hiding place, and you to yours. But a gift for your courage."

The crone's hand felt warm on her face for just a moment before it disappeared, leaving Euryale cold and shaking.

"The Water Goddess prides herself on her gifts of prophecy. And so I gift them to you. May they help you keep the ones you love safe from this day on."

The older woman started to hobble away. With the last of her strength, Euryale managed to whisper, "Wait. Who are you?"

The crone gave a lopsided grin and said, "I have many names and none. Go and live."

~

Euryale attempted to shove these memories down and away as she usually did, but no matter how she tried, her past stirred within her mind, making her more irritable by the moment.

The insufferable stranger she was tracking had a good lead on her. He'd been letting her follow before, it seemed. Her snakes licked the air around her, as agitated as she was.

He'd gone beyond the border of her lands. It would be dangerous for her to follow. The Beasts and Creatures that resided under the great canopy of trees in the Beast Realm wouldn't bat an eye at slaying Euryale should she be discovered outside her territory.

Euryale hesitated. The stranger had said he was going toward the stream. She wondered if his new plan was to circle her lands and then cut back through to the stream he'd been making his way toward. If that was the case, she could cut him off and head straight there. But what if he was up to something else?

What if it was a trap, and the moment she went to head him off, he went back to the cavern and finished off her sisters?

She had no choice but to follow, and so, for the first time in a long time, Euryale slithered across the territory boundary.

It wasn't as if the trees or the ground were any different from one movement to the next, but the scent in the air changed. It smelled of wild woods and Beasts, their odor and claw marks everywhere.

It sent a shiver of fear down her spine. It was one thing when they came looking for trouble in her lands. It was another for her to be willingly gliding into their clutches.

The forest around her disappeared, and the same prophecy she'd had before took hold.

Blood, screams, chaos.

Her sisters were dead. Medusa's head was being held up like a trophy while her red Gorgon blood burned holes in the floor of the cavern. The male holding her head, smiling, was not the green-eyed Creature Euryale had been hunting.

It was a clear enough vision to know it would happen soon. Euryale would arrive far too late. The bodies would be stiff with death by the time she returned. She didn't have much time. This was the path that would befall her sisters, thanks to the choice she was making now.

Euryale turned to return to the cavern, and again another vision washed over her. Not much better than the first, except she'd be arriving just as the group of males, Shifters perhaps, or Halflings, were leaving.

They'd catch her, too, just outside the cavern.

But what choice did she have but to go back, even if it was useless?

Her eyes drifted for a moment toward the stream. The stranger she'd been afraid would ruin them was of no consequence. She and her sisters had brought this down on themselves. Foolish to think that others could ever learn to fear them. All they did was hate them for their monstrous forms.

Euryale didn't know what made her risk the precious seconds, but she did, turning and moving slightly forward, toward the stream. She knew her prophecies were never wrong. Sometimes they were misguided, the ending not being exactly as it had initially appeared to be, but no less accurate unless something changed the line of fate.

Euryale realized her mistake. She'd almost killed the Creature that could be the only one to save her sisters.

She wasted no time cutting through the trees, cursing herself inwardly for not learning his name. Still, he'd known she was trailing him before. He hadn't needed light. What were the odds his hearing wasn't spot on? He'd hear her coming. Would it be enough?

He was a dark, shadowed blur, moving swiftly before her.

"I need your help!" she screamed, words she'd never thought she'd say to anyone, let alone a man.

She and her sisters were proud. They could take care of themselves usually. But Euryale had seen no other course to save them but this one. As much as the words burned like acid in her mouth, they were true. She needed help, and he was the only one that could provide it.

He stilled and turned, looking over his shoulder at the sound of her voice.

"Please. It's my sisters."

He turned and continued going. Euryale decided she was going to kill him if he didn't help her. She crashed through the trees, trying to catch up with him, but he was fast, so much faster than she'd ever suspected.

He was gone, lost to her vision completely. It was so startling that even the snakes of her hair were frantically licking, not understanding where he'd gone and how he'd gone so quickly.

Of course he wouldn't help her. What man ever had? Still, it wasn't anger that engulfed her but fear and despair. She screamed and fell to her knees as the last vision overtook her.

With their only chance of help gone, it was too horrible to see. They were things she'd seen before. She'd face her fate and her failure. But oh, what pain it would be. Her sisters lying dead beside her.

Her visions were never wrong, but the outcomes could still change, maybe if she hurried, maybe.

His voice sounded next to her, as if he'd materialized at her side from the shadows themselves.

"Tell me, and quickly, so I can decide."

His words were harsh and brutal. Why shouldn't they be? She and her sisters had tried repeatedly to kill him. And now here she was, bent low in the dirt, hardly able to draw breath for the fear that clutched her.

Why would he care to help her? Why would he care for her pain?

"Men," she said the word like spitting poison. "They're going to kill them. They're already on the way, and I can't stop them, and neither can my sisters. There are too many, and there's too much hatred. It will be a bloodbath."

"That's not my concern," the stranger said as he took a step away from her.

"Please," she hated the word.

Euryale hated that she was going to beg and bargain and plead. But she would. She'd do anything.

"Anything that you want. Name it, and it's yours. Just please, help them."

"How many will I have to kill?"

"So many I couldn't count them all."

The stranger stared down at her. His green eyes were hard and unflinching as gem rocks. He had no love for her or her sisters. It seemed as if he had no love at all for the world around him either. And yet he stood, and yet he stayed.

With a snarl of his lips, he asked, "How do you know?"

"I have visions. I've seen it. They're prophetic, a gift, but with visions like these, it's more a curse."

He raised his dark eyebrows, and she could've sworn there was a slight flicker of a smile as he said, "I know a thing or two about prophecies. Follow behind as quickly as you can."

The Creature disappeared a moment later.

She couldn't believe it and stayed stunned on the ground where she was for a moment. A man helping her? It felt as if the world were turning upside down.

Another vision flooded her senses. There was blood, blood everywhere, and a stench so strong she could almost smell it. Soon she would, and soon she'd pay the price for this help. However, the price wasn't at all what Euryale was expecting it to be.

~

It had taken Euryale and her sisters several days to find a suitable new cavern. To deal with the heap of bodies piled within their old one had been too much work.

Bloodstains dripped from the walls and pooled on the floor. The smell lingered thick and heavy in the air.

By the time she'd arrived, moving as quickly she could, the stranger was long gone. Her sisters had sat stunned in the corner by the corpses, both of their faces covered in gore and blood. Yet there wasn't a single scratch on them.

Euryale had pulled them out of the cavern and taken them to a shallow stream nearby. As she scrubbed away blood and bits of flesh, the story had come loose from her sisters.

Males from a nearby Shifter clan had come in their Human forms, thinking to find them easy prey, wanting to retake the Gorgon territory as their own.

"They were all sated with drink," Medusa whispered. "Cruel, with so much anger in their hearts."

"They showed up so quickly we didn't have time to escape the cavern," Stheno added softly.

They'd come with shields to cover their eyes and thick leather wrapped around their necks to keep Stheno's blades from them. Medusa only had her eyes as her gift. Otherwise, she was weak. Without any of them stupid enough to look at her, they'd been overwhelmed.

And then the stranger had rampaged through the cavern, shaking the walls while flames licked the entrance.

They spoke of him in soft, hushed voices, but Euryale didn't think it was fear she heard there but awe.

She had to admit the tale they painted was impressive. The stranger had dispatched the men quickly, felling one, twisting on another. Using their weapons against them, using each other's swords to fell their comrades. He strangled several with the leather that was supposed to protect them.

When the last one died, her sisters said the stranger's sword clattered to the ground. He looked at them, and her sisters admitted in hushed tones that they'd been terrified of him for that split second, bathed in blood and gore as he was.

But then he nodded and turned, walking through the flames that extinguished as he passed, and by the time the smoke had cleared, he was gone, not a trace to be seen.

THE GORGON AND THE STRANGER

Once Euryale had gotten the story and had seen the bodies for herself, she realized how clever the stranger had been. Using the aggressors' own weapons against them, no one could blame him or the Gorgons.

When the Shifters had been upon her sisters, they'd loudly stated that they'd announced to their clan that they were going Gorgon hunting. They'd crowed with the prefabricated victory of returning to their clan with Gorgon heads.

It was easy to remove the few items she and her sisters possessed from the cavern. Several of the Shifters had come with bottles of liquor still in hand, and the sisters had strategically moved them around the cavern.

By the time she and her sisters had stood at the cavern entrance, Euryale almost smiled. It looked like a drunken brawl of rowdy Shifters and nothing more. Hopped up on drink and anger as they'd been, their weapons and blood would sing the story that they'd slaughtered each other.

She and her sisters left the cavern that they'd made their home and retreated to one not far from it. Still within their territory, they resettled.

The sisters stayed far enough away from the cavern filled with bodies not to draw notice, but they saw all.

Not often did others come creeping into their section of the trees, but the sisters let the scavengers in this time. The Chupacabra and several carnivorous Shifters slowly dragged off bodies, further muddying any sign of them from the scene.

The predators they heard a long way off and stayed hidden in the darkness of their cavern and the shadows of the trees. The Shifters from the clan that had attacked them were a discomfort, but the sisters suffered as a few brave ones ventured into their forest to collect a dead friend or relative.

The living spread the story of the dead as they dragged the corpses behind them.

"I've never seen anything like it," one said as he hauled a son or grandson by the ankles past Euryale's hiding spot. "The bunch of drunken fools killed each other."

"You don't think it was the Gorgons?" one of the boys asked, dragging a corpse by its arms.

"Nah," the first one said. "Not a single one turned to stone, not a single one sliced through the throat or crushed. These idiots did it to themselves. But we better get out of here before the Gorgons start tracking us. Now, hurry."

~

Euryale had known when the stranger would return since she'd seen it in her vision. Still, when it happened, it made her heart race and her snakes quiver. Never had she thought such a thing would be possible.

When she'd told her sisters, they'd hardly believed it to be true. But Euryale had assured them she'd seen it that day as clear as glass through the shape of time.

The stranger slowly sauntered into their new cavern and looked around with his reflective green eyes.

"It's not as nice as the other one. Apologies that you had to move."

She and her sisters sat still, as if they were made of stone themselves. She knew what would happen next, but it was so unbelievable to her that Euryale could hardly wrap her mind around it, let alone bring it to fruition.

Medusa, her beautiful sister, would never learn. Men had hurt her and deceived her. They'd cursed her, and yet, despite all that, Euryale was sure somewhere in her sister's heart, she loved them still. She and Stheno would never love men the way her Medusa did.

It was their youngest sister, with her beautiful face, who smiled and beckoned the stranger further inside.

"Thank you for saving us," she said softly, almost shyly.

"You should thank your sister," the stranger said, surprising them all as he came and sat beside Euryale. "If it weren't for her, I never would've helped."

She was stunned speechless. An honest man was almost as unbelievable as what the future would hold for them.

"We have thanked her," Stheno said with a disapproving frown. "She said you'd return, but what we don't know is why."

The stranger turned, lifting his brows in silent question, and asked, "Another prophecy?"

"A vision of the days and years to come. Are you here for repayment?" Euryale asked.

The man shrugged his shoulders with fluid grace. "My repayment should be one that you see fit. I don't know what it will be or when you'll repay me. But somewhere down the line, you will. You owe me, Euryale. And owing someone a life debt is a powerful thing."

She nodded, feeling a spike of curiosity sing through her veins. This one was strange and broken too. He was perhaps like them, with a history and a past or future he was trying to outrun.

Words fell from his lips, but almost painfully, as if he was unused to using them. There had been a time when Euryale and her sisters had felt the same.

"I should know to whom I owe my debts. A name to call a friend would be helpful."

Euryale hesitated using the word friend, but that was what they'd be. She and her sisters would befriend this stranger. She'd seen him coming and going, him learning to confide in them, and them in him.

He'd save them several more times in the years to come and help them more than anyone they'd ever known or would ever know.

This strange Creature would be one that she'd grow to care for, not as a lover, for she'd never allow another man to touch her again. But as a friend, as a companion, as someone as reeling and broken by the world as they'd been. Friends were what they'd be from the day they'd met until her last. They'd be friends.

"My name is Atanas, but you can call me Tase."

~

Tase and the Gorgons will return again in *Through the Silent Forest*.

A Sneak Peak of Through the Silent Forest
PART ONE
Chapter One

Diana had been lying awake, staring at the shadowed ceiling of her bedroom for what felt like a lifetime. She had been sound asleep earlier, exhausted from the day's work, when fears of what was to come jolted her awake, making her heart hammer in her chest. Now, all those fears were running rampant through her mind.

Diana knew that the ceremony that would take place tomorrow was something that she could never change. There was no reason to fear it or to shy away from her destiny. She had always been meant to be chief, and tomorrow was the day she'd take her rightful place among her people.

It wasn't a surprise, and it wasn't particularly terrifying either. Diana had been groomed for this position for as long as she could remember. But the anxiety that she'd felt growing steadily in the pit of her stomach had increased to an overwhelming intensity over the past week.

No matter how hard Diana tried, sleep eluded her. Though she closed her eyes and willed herself to do so, she couldn't seem to manage it. It didn't matter how she fluffed her pillow or adjusted herself on the comfortable bed with her favorite blanket. She couldn't relax. Her foot darted out from under the blanket, only to be drawn back in a moment later. Finally, she sighed and sat up.

Diana's long black curling hair had strands sticking out of her knotted bun that fell in front of her face. Without thought, she undid the knot and retied it.

Diana had attempted to speak to her parents and grandmother about her feelings, but every time she'd tried, the words caught in her throat. It wasn't the ceremony that she feared but what came after. She knew what was expected of her in some ways, but she was completely unsure of what to do in other aspects. Now, the night before her big day, it was much too late to try to back out of anything.

Ridiculous, she thought as she rubbed her eyes. *You're being ridiculous.*

No matter how ridiculous Diana felt, she couldn't rest. She needed peace of mind, and the only way to do that was to seek help far beyond herself. Without lighting the candle by her bed, Diana walked across her bedroom to the chair in the corner. It held her work clothes for the next day. She shrugged out of her long white sleeping gown, throwing it lazily across her unmade bed.

Diana put on the plain brown dress and reached for her cloak hanging from a peg next to the chair. She pulled the cloak over her shoulders, fastening the worn brass clasps, and tugged the hood up over her head. As silently as she could, she crept from her bedroom.

Diana's room on the castle's first floor was the only one occupied in the small hallway. To the right, around the bend of the hall, the gardeners and their families lived. She turned to the left, walking the few paces to the garden door.

She clasped the handle and swung the door open slowly. Diana's heart was hammering in her chest. The last thing she needed was to be caught doing something she wasn't supposed to do. And sneaking out of the castle in the middle of the night was something her parents would nag her about all day, telling her she knew better and that they, as always, expected better from her.

Diana went in and out of this doorway every morning. She knew that it squeaked loudly right before opening fully. Diana opened the door enough to slip her slender body through, stopping the door before it squeaked. She stood poised in the doorframe, listening for the sounds of the guards. She soon heard the scuff of boots and tucked herself into the shadows as they passed by.

"I'm hoping to get a few hours of sleep after my shift ends. Then I'll join the festivities."

Diana recognized Joshua's low, even tone as he spoke to his fellow guard. As the pair passed over the garden walkway, they paused. Diana shrank back, fearing they'd turn and spot her.

"Me too," Jonah, the younger of the two, replied. "Emily's so excited. She's been driving me crazy, talking about the ceremony nonstop. She even made a new dress, special for the occasion. But honestly, I just can't wait to eat all the food after the announcement. My mom's been telling me all about the pies they are baking special for it," he said, sighing as they turned toward Castleton.

Their backs were to her, their eyes pinned on the small, rambling town outside the castle's gates. Diana breathed a sigh of relief but silently willed them to keep walking.

"I've been smelling the food all night. It's making me miserable," Joshua said with a good-natured laugh. "We can eat soon enough."

The guards turned, marching down the rest of the garden walk and then up the steps that connected them to the castle wall.

Once their footsteps faded away, Diana floated across the garden. Her light steps were long and confident. Before Diana knew it, she was standing beside the dark rose bushes. Creeping around the large plants she was next to, Diana snagged her gardening shears and snipped off a single white rose. Tucking it into her pocket, she turned silently to the garden gate, which led out into the forest.

With a quick turn of her head to make sure no other guards were near, Diana darted out of the garden gate and into the dark forest beyond. Once she was in the woods, the scent of pine and sycamore soothed her turbulent soul, and she smiled.

Diana's feet knew the way. Her mind ran again and again over the chiefing ceremony that would take place in just a few short hours. She needed someone who'd hear her and listen to her without judgment or consequence.

Diana picked her way through the trees and moss until she found the path that led to her destination. The forest had always been one of her favorite places. The tall trees were as familiar to her as the paths on which her feet walked. She'd constantly used them to escape her day-to-day life. As often as she could, Diana would sit beneath the safety of the trees and read.

Her grandmother had told her, long ago, when the world had been different, that there had been Dryads and Nymphs that lived as souls inside the trees. There had also been Fae, who bonded with trees, and trees made of magic that spoke and moved on their own.

Diana smiled, touching the trees gently as she passed. She knew the tales were from long before her time, but she loved them.

It was the darkest part of the night. Satisfied that she'd have plenty of time, Diana pulled her cloak tighter around her shoulders and trudged on. She'd need to be back before anyone realized she was gone. She shivered, thinking of the scene that would play out if her family found her missing and all the fuss that would erupt on her account.

I can't let that happen, she thought. *It won't take that long.*

Her feet guided her along the forest path with ease as she came to the place where the dirt path widened into a cut and cleared circle. Inside the circle stood a shrine. It was an ancient stone carving raised on a dais. Her grandmother had told her that the statues had been carved long before Terrene had even become a country.

The statue had been cleaned and polished in the last few days; Diana could tell as it glimmered in the starlight. The God's outstretched arms were cobweb free, and all the dirt had been brushed away from the base. A multitude of red and yellow flowers was arranged about the bottom of the dais.

Diana approached the statue slowly, cautiously, as if it was a living, breathing thing. She knelt in the dirt before the statue, lowering herself into a postulant state as she took the rose from her pocket. Holding it out before her, with her forehead touching the ground, Diana began.

"I know that you won't be angry," she whispered, her voice soft and beseeching as her eyes shut tight as the statue began to glow. "I needed you. I need your help."

Diana tilted her head up and kissed the feet of the statue. Then she placed the white rose atop a yellow daisy and sat up, letting the glow shine upon her face.

Diana peered up into the faceless form of the cloaked and shrouded God. Although the carving of his face had long ago worn away, she could see eyes watching her. Diana could see him, the God she loved, looking down on her, judging her, and weighing her words. She could feel him all around in this sacred place, which was his and his alone.

"Please. Please help me," she begged the unflinching face of the God.

"I don't know what to do, and I can't ask anyone else. They won't understand why it's such a big deal, why I won't just be able to choose, why I already haven't decided. I can't ask anyone else to guide me but you. You're the God of Love, after all. If anyone knows how to help me, it's you."

A sense of peace and understanding settled upon her shoulders, caressing her with the God's love. Diana closed her eyes and felt the brush of the breeze against her cheek. She smiled as she opened her eyes.

With the sense of peace settling inside her chest, Diana realized that she should've come sooner. She should've implored the God before all her worries had set in.

"Thank you. I'll do it. I'll choose someone. I know I'll have to, and I'll try to pick the person who's the best, not just for me, but for Terrene too. I won't fail my country. But you know my true heart, and I know that you'll lead me where I need to go."

He had plans for her, as all the Gods did. But this God, more than any other, except maybe the Mother Goddess, held a special place in Diana's heart. The God of Death and Love knew all her secrets. This God knew that, though she'd do as she was expected to after the ceremony, it wasn't what her heart wanted.

Diana had grown up on stories of wild creatures and adventures. She'd grown up on love stories. That was what she wanted. She wanted adventure and epic romance. She didn't want to be forced, to have to choose, not when she wasn't even sure she knew what love like that was.

She closed her eyes, and when she opened them again, the light of the statue had faded back to cold, dark stone.

Diana stood, brushing the dirt off her dress, and then wiped her hands clean on it. She took one of the God's outreached hands in her own, squeezing the solid stone as if bidding a friend farewell. She was just about to turn around when a throat cleared behind her.

Diana winced, dreading how she was going to explain herself.

"Sorry to disturb you," Joshua said softly from behind her. "But we need to begin lighting the ceremonial torches. The sun's almost up, and the townspeople will be coming to pray for the new chief."

Joshua's voice sounded hesitant. Interrupting people's prayers was rude. Diana stilled and nodded. If he'd heard her voice or her prayers, he gave no indication. She silently thanked the God of Death for her good fortune.

Tugging the cloak further over her face, Diana turned so that she was angled away from the guard and picked up her pace, moving away from the statue. She heard others coming down the path. Gardeners and workers carried torches, burning away the night and lighting the way to the God of Love and Death.

~

"So, who can tell me what happened after the War of the Siblings?" Diana asked as she stopped writing on the chalkboard and turned to face her students.

Small, eager hands shot up, and several tiny voices said, "Oh, I know," and, "Pick me, pick me."

Diana's brown eyes darted quickly from one student to another. She had a small classroom of about eight children, ranging from ages eight to ten. Their dirt-smudged, happy faces were beaming up at her the same as they did every week when she taught history for a few hours as part of her routine. She smiled at them.

"Daniel is sitting very quietly with his hand raised," Diana announced as her eyes landed on the small eight-year-old boy with untidy black hair. "Daniel, why don't you tell us what happened after the War of the Siblings?"

Daniel puffed up his chest with pride and answered in a high-pitched little voice. "After the war, we built Terrene. We made the castle inside and made the walls. And then, and then, we put up watches and guards on the towers to make sure our enemies stay away."

"Yes," Diana said. "You're correct. But, who can tell me something else that happened after the War of the Siblings?"

The children's hands shot up, but this time their voices were quiet.

"Anna, why don't you tell the class what else happened?"

Anna, with a mouth full of missing teeth, confidently answered, "We signed the contract for no more war. The children of the Earth Goddess Terra promised not to fight each other anymore."

"Yes, exactly. Excellent," Diana said as she nodded encouragingly. Then, turning her body halfway, she pointed to the map on the wall behind her. "As you can see here, after the War of the Siblings ended, and the contract was signed, all the peoples who'd been previously spread out across Panterra had to separate. The Dragons and all their Beast kind went here," Diana said, pointing to the rocky eastern terrain on the map, to the Land of the Beasts. "Who can tell me where the Fae went?"

Hands shot up, and eager faces smiled. Diana pointed to Cesar and nodded for him to answer.

"They went to the west, and the Vampires and the Undead went to the north."

"Very good," Diana said, "very good. It seems you've all been studying incredibly hard. Now, who can tell me about the Merpeople?

Who can tell me how we're protected against them when we have shores and streams of water here in Terrene?" Diana asked her class.

But her question would go unanswered because just as the last words fell from her lips, the door to the schoolroom opened. Her grandmother's kind face and braided gray hair came into view. All the children's eyes darted guiltily between Diana and her grandmother.

"I thought I might find you here. I believe Alexander was supposed to be teaching this lesson while you were getting ready for your big ceremony in just a few hours," Raini said, looking at her granddaughter. Though her voice was reproachful, her eyes were smiling.

If anyone else in her family had caught her, Diana would've had to explain why she was doing something she wasn't supposed to be doing. It was true Alexander should've been teaching this lesson, but she'd told him not to come. It was her last lesson with the children, after all, the last routine event that she'd done day in and day out for years.

But her grandmother knew her best of all. Diana had every day from before dawn to well after dusk packed with chores, lessons, and obligations that she needed to fulfill. On the rare occasion, she'd have a few hours to herself. But what was she supposed to do with an entire morning?

Her grandmother's eyes were the same as Diana's, brown as melted chocolate. They slid from Diana to the class of silent, sullen children.

"I'm sorry to break up this history lesson. But, as you know, Diana has an eventful afternoon. The class is dismissed," her grandmother's tone brooked no room for argument.

The children, seated cross-legged on the swept stone floor, stood but weren't eager to go. Anna, the little girl with missing teeth, took it upon herself to voice the one question they were all keen to know.

"Are you nervous, Diana?"

Diana ran a quick hand over the little girl's hair and answered, "A little bit. But it's always been meant to be for me to take my place among our people. And you can't be afraid of your destiny."

The little girl's head nodded as if she understood the weight of Diana's answer.

Then Lucas, a quiet and shy little boy, said, "My mama said we're going to be there for the ceremony, not just the feast."

"Good," Diana answered, smiling and trying to keep the tears from her eyes. "I hope that all of you will come. It's a good part of your history lessons."

Then, clearing the tears from her voice, she said, "Next week's lesson will begin right where we left off today, but with Alexander. I expect all of you to be excellent students for him, just as you've been for me. So, be sure to keep studying with your parents and make me proud. Now, off with you all; my grandmother won't be kept waiting."

The children giggled at the sight of the older woman standing silently in the doorway, tapping her foot. They hugged Diana, wishing her well and leaving as slowly as possible.

Raini, the retired chief of Terrene and Diana's grandmother, pushed them out the door and down the hall.

Once the room was clear of children, Diana, not eager to leave either, began erasing the chalkboard and then jotted a quick note to Alexander, her friend who'd be taking over the children's lessons from here on out. She had just finished signing it when her grandmother came back, wearing a harassed expression on her face.

"You can't stall much longer. Your mother is having a fit," Raini informed Diana with no little glee. "Let's get you up there before she sends the guards to drag you," Raini added, offering an arm to her granddaughter.

Diana took it, and the two of them made their way down the hall, past the other classrooms and the library. Then they turned up a staircase leading to the northern tower of the castle. Diana's grandmother, sensing her nerves, began to chat about a book that she was reading. Diana, only half listening, still lost in her thoughts, nodded at all the right places and made appreciative noises, as she should, though her heart wasn't in it.

Much sooner than she would've thought possible, Diana had reached the door that led to the base of her mother's rooms. Without giving her granddaughter time to run back down the stairs, Raini pushed the door open. Diana heard her mother's imperious tone from within.

"No. No. No. I told Noah that I wanted white roses with blue forget-me-nots sprinkled inside, not the other way around. Tell him to fix it and to be quick about it. I need the centerpieces on the tables in the hall before the ceremony starts."

Lydia, Diana's mother's friend and assistant, nodded eagerly, taking away the affronting flowers with a delicacy that few possessed. "Of course. While I'm down there, I'll check in on the kitchen as well. I can give you an update when I get back." Lydia squeezed Diana's mother's arm and said softly, "It's going to be okay. Everything will be beautiful, you'll see."

Diana's mother, Arabella, co-chief of Terrene, didn't so much as smile back at her friend as her dark, almost black stern eyes drifted to her daughter and mother-in-law standing in the doorway. "I see you found her. And where was she?" Diana's mother asked as if Diana wasn't standing there in the room with them.

With a kind smile, Raini answered, "The classroom. Where else?"

Arabella rolled her eyes, then, setting her steely gaze on her daughter, said, "You know better. I have been out of my mind, Diana. Simply out of my mind with everything that I have to do for today, and where were you? Doing nothing. Teaching children who won't remember a thing after they've left you. And seriously, Diana, of all days to go running off, you had to choose today. Really?" Arabella asked, talking more to herself than her daughter.

Diana swallowed her sigh of agitation. Her grandmother had known exactly where she was. The same place she'd been every week at this time. Her mother was just being dramatic because she hadn't been in her room. But Diana didn't need hours to get ready. If she'd had it her way, she would've just changed into the special dress, checked that there was no chalk on her face, and have done with it. But that would've horrified her mother.

Arabella motioned with an impatient hand gesture for Diana to come in and shut the door behind her. Diana reluctantly stepped into her mother's perfumed salon. The room, adorned with comfortable couches and a small, low table, was meant to be welcoming, but it had always made Diana feel nervous. There was a tray of assorted cured meats, hard cheeses, and fruits. Next to it, in a slim bucket from the underground cellars, was a bottle of pear juice.

"You don't have time to eat now," Arabella informed Diana as Raini sat on a sofa and popped a grape into her mouth. "You have to get ready. We are out of time. Go to my bathroom. I'll be there in just a moment."

Without waiting for her daughter to answer, Arabella turned to Raini and began prattling about the food and the procession. Diana turned away and wandered through the open doorway into her mother's bathroom. She sighed in relief, pleased to have gotten away for the moment. Her mother had gone over the ceremony again and again. It wasn't as if things weren't set already, as if there was any stopping it now.

Diana peeled off the work dress she'd put on long before the sun had risen and got into the tub. The water was tepid, another sign that her mother had been expecting her some time ago. She felt terrible for all the workers who had to heat the water and carry it up the endless flights to her mother's chamber, just for her to dirty it.

If it had been any other day, Diana would've gone to the bathing house, filled with warm pools of sulfurous water. But today wasn't just any day. No matter how Diana had tried to put off thinking about it and stalled, there was no use anymore.

She dipped her head below the surface of the water, letting all sounds and thoughts drift away. Her racing heart slowed, and her limbs loosened. When she came back up for air, there was no more peace. Her mother was standing in the doorway, eyeing her with a knowing glance.

"The water is filthy, Diana. What have you been doing? Were you mucking the stables this morning?" Arabella asked tartly as she came to the back side of the tub and plunked down the small stool she'd been carrying with her. Seated by her daughter's head, she commanded, "Soap."

Obediently, Diana reached for the bar of lavender honey soap, handing it to her mother. Like the rest of the family, Arabella was stressed, but much more than any of the others. Diana knew it was because her mother, unlike her, hadn't been born into the role of chief but had married into it. Therefore, she made up for it in every way she could, though no one had ever asked her to.

With little thought for her daughter's peace of mind, Arabella scrubbed Diana's skin until it was red. The sand in the soap scratched, but Diana made not a sound as her mother, who didn't need to scrub her, but had insisted upon it, went about her work.

The two women, lost in their thoughts, went through the motions. Diana was scrubbed clean; her hair was washed, oiled, and scented. Then she was whisked from the tub and patted down. Her hair was wrapped in a drying cloth and her body in another. Arabella had worked in steely silence while they'd been in the bathroom, but Diana had known that it was too good to last.

"Diana," her mother said in a sharp tone that set her teeth on edge. "There's something that we must discuss. I've asked your grandmother to stay, to help me explain."

Chapter Two

Diana stood, shaking, just inside the castle's walls. The main wooden gate was thrown open wide. She could see the people lining both sides of the path she'd walk. The people of Terrene were silently waiting, watching. The only sound was the beating of the drum, pounding low and menacing from somewhere before her. Standing alone, Diana took a deep breath to calm herself and took her first step forward.

The steady beat of the drum pounding in rhythm to her walk eased the tightness in her chest as she took one step after another. She couldn't look left or right, only before her, ahead of her, at what was to come. Diana couldn't see the end of the path yet. The procession spanned from the castle's main gate all the way to the shrine of the Mother Goddess Terra. The shrine was invisible to Diana from this distance, but what was visible was her little brother.

Sancus, who was only six years old, walked in front of her. She could tell by the set of his shoulders that he was excited. His little head turned from side to side eagerly. Just the thought of moving her eyes made Diana feel nauseous.

A radiant smile played on Sancus's lips for all that looked his way. He had on the traditional green and brown that all children of Terrene wore. Their mother had sewn him pants made of leather. The green shirt he wore was made of the softest silk, embroidered with golden thread. Sancus looked just like every child born in Terrene; he was the embodiment of their people, with his suntanned skin, dark, raven-colored hair, and chocolate eyes.

Her little brother, breaking the rules as always, turned his head to look back at his sister. Seeing Diana's steely expression of determination as she walked, he quickly turned back around.

In front of Sancus walked their parents, keeping pace as Diana did with the drums. Their heads didn't turn. They walked like Gods made of stone, her mother on the right, and her father on the left, walking arm in arm down the long procession of silent onlookers.

Arabella wore a dress in the traditional green that all women wore for all special occasions to honor the Mother Goddess. Her long, straight hair was worn down, as was the custom.

Diana's eyes drifted to the crown of feathers on her father's headdress. As acting chief, Julius wore one made of all white feathers. The headdress flowed halfway down his back. His black hair, braided, came down past his waist, ending with a single white feather. His supple brown clothes were plain and unadorned. The chief, tall and robust with his headdress, was all that the people needed him to be.

Diana knew that beyond him walked her grandmother, leading the family procession. She'd seen Raini only a few minutes before, but it felt like a lifetime as Diana walked down the path surrounded by staring people. Her grandmother wore a plain gray dress and the black headdress of the spiritual leaders.

Diana's mind had focused on the tiny details of her family, their dress and their steps as they moved through the crowd of people toward their destination. Now, as they drew closer to the statue, she could hardly think of anything at all. Her mind had gone blank with the drumming. Although Diana's heart was fluttering wildly with excitement, terror raged through her.

Diana could feel the people's eyes on her, and just as she was about to turn her head and look at them, she saw her parents begin to slow their pace. Behind them, Sancus slowed dutifully, following their lead. Then her grandmother stopped, and her parents, brother, and finally she followed, as the drums ceased.

Raini was standing on the foot of the dais, facing her granddaughter and her people. The older woman's face was painted white, making her look like a wild thing made of spirit. Behind Raini stood the statue of Terra, the Mother Goddess of Earth and Creation.

THE GORGON AND THE STRANGER

Raini stood with her hands out before her. Diana saw her parents split apart. They turned, facing her, and stood on either side of her grandmother.

Arabella's face looked ashen and sickly. Julius's white-painted face, matching his mother's, gave Diana a radiant smile. It settled the roiling, excited emotions in her stomach.

Diana's little brother turned, joining their mother. Diana saw Arabella's hand tremble as she set it lightly on Sancus's shoulder, pulling him into place.

"People of Terrene!" Raini announced to the crowd that had assembled behind the family, closing behind Diana as she'd passed them.

Every man, woman, and child drew in close to hear.

Only Raini's powerful voice sounded through the quiet of the forest. It seemed as if even the birds, animals, and wind itself held their breath as they listened and waited.

"Today is a joyous day, not only for my family, with a coming of age ceremony, but for all our people! Today we rejoice! Today we thank the Goddess of Creation and Life for gifting Terrene with a new chieftain."

With the words *new chieftain*, the swarm of people around Diana cheered, clapped, and stomped their feet. They called out to Diana with joyous voices. She felt their delight engulfing her. But her face was set, stern and emotionless, as her mother had reminded continuously her to do. Diana looked now, not at her father beaming with pride, but at her grandmother's steady, unwavering brown eyes.

"Come, daughter of Terra," Raini said.

The crowd silenced once again, going deathly still as Diana stepped forward to the foot of the dais and knelt before her grandmother.

Diana wore a dress that she'd wear twice in her life, as every female chief had done before her. Her dress was made of all white silk. It flowed, hanging loosely around her, pooling and tucking in just the right places to make her look beautiful. Around her waist was a garland of green vines twisted with white blooming roses. Her long, curling black hair cascaded behind her back.

As Diana knelt, she unconsciously tucked her hair behind her ear. The white dress was instantly smudged with dirt as her knees touched the ground.

Here, just as at the other clearing, with the God of Death, Diana felt the Goddess' presence. It didn't shine but seeped through the ground, up her legs, through her veins, and into her heart. The small white flowers planted at the base of the statue opened.

Diana sighed, feeling the blessing of the Goddess upon her. She heard the collective sigh of the people of Terrene around her. The mantle of chief was passed down upon the eighteenth birthday of each female descendant. In cases like her father's, where he was an only child, it had passed to him. But even then, they had to seek the Goddess's approval. The blooming flowers were a sign for all to see the Goddess's favor.

"Diana, daughter of Julius, do you swear on your life's blood to protect the country of Terrene?" Raini asked, her voice amplified with emotion.

Diana bent her head in supplication and calmly stated, "I do."

"And do you promise, on the lifeblood of your family, to keep Terrene in peace and harmony from this day until the end of days?"

"I do."

"And lastly, do you, Diana, daughter of Julius, accept that you are Terrene, the blood and life force of Terrene, and as such, wish to become chieftain and rule justly and fairly for all the days of your life?"

The crowd was silent. The forest held its breath. Mother Terra, asleep, deep within the earth, waited for one, then two heartbeats.

Diana looked up to see the worn face of the Goddess of Creation and answered proudly, "Yes. I do."

Raini nodded, and Julius moved, holding out a bowl filled with white paint. Her grandmother dipped both thumbs into it, drawing a half circle on Diana's forehead with each of her fingers.

With grave solemnity, Raini stated, "So that the God of the Sun may shine upon every day that you rule."

Diana shuddered as the cold paint touched her skin. Raini then dipped her index and middle fingers into the paint.

"So that the God of Death and Love may guide you when you are lost," Raini said gently as she dragged her fingers simultaneously down, like tears running from Diana's eyes to her chin. Then, placing her ring fingers in the paint, Raini put two drops of paint on Diana's chin.

"So that the Goddess Terra will keep you grounded and humble."

Lastly, Raini took her pinkies, thick with white paint, and gave Diana horizontal half-circles under each eye.

"So that the Goddess of Water may open your eyes that you may always see the truth and judge in fairness."

Diana's breath was ragged. She felt as if she couldn't breathe. Hurriedly, Diana blinked back tears of joy that were threatening to ruin her ceremonial paint. While her eyes were closed, Raini adorned her with the final piece that would make her chief.

Diana knew it without seeing it. It settled on her head, heavy as the burden she would bear for her people as chief, but not too heavy to bend her strength. The headdress had been made especially for her, consisting of white feathers with black tips artfully arranged. Diana's fear and emotion melted away as it settled into place.

Taking Raini's hand and standing smoothly, Diana twirled out from her grandmother, facing the multitude of people. The people of Terrene were cheering, whistling, and shouting with joy. It washed over Diana, as cleansing as the sea, washing away everything that she was and everything that she'd been, making her new, making her chieftain.

~

The hall was hot with stagnant air. The fiery torches, spaced every few feet on the walls, only seemed to add to the problem. Though the windows were all thrown open, and the sun had long set, the room held too many people.

After the ceremony, the onlookers had returned to feast at the castle. The food that had been in preparation for days was laid out. The smell of roasted meats, sweet sauces, and ripe fruit hung in the air.

Diana's people were happy, celebrating, and giving toasts. Several swayed as they enjoyed the rhythmic beat of drums that floated in through the windows. Diana was happy, but she didn't celebrate with them. She smiled with each cheer for her, laughed, talked, and greeted people as they passed. But all she wanted to do was be alone, and yet she couldn't.

Some time ago, Diana had escaped to the back of the hall, sinking quietly into the long shadows that the torches left between them. She stood by the food, murmuring pleasantries to anyone who came up.

Diana was right next to all her favorite foods, but she hadn't touched a thing all evening. The thought of taking a bite of anything made her feel queasy all over again.

She watched the hall, as she always did during meals. Diana watched the faces that passed her, noted the clothing and the actions of her people. A young couple had her attention now. They were kissing and holding hands for all to see. They seemed to be enjoying themselves very much in a corner across the room. Diana was lost in thought, imagining with equal dread and delight what it would be like to kiss someone like that in front of everyone.

Before today, things like kissing had been forbidden to her. As the future chief, Diana's family had set strict rules. She wasn't allowed to be alone with boys in her room. She wasn't allowed to hold hands or do anything that might be unseemly, yet now that she was eighteen, now that she was crowned as chief, that would all change very quickly.

Diana blinked and backed away, startled as a plate materialized before her. The smell was what had drawn her distracted attention, warm apple pie topped with cinnamon and dusted with sparkling dark sugar. It was one of her favorites. Stunned, she looked stupidly down at the plate.

Diana heard Malakai's voice in her ear, "I've been watching you all night. You haven't eaten a thing." Diana smiled up at her best friend as he moved into view, but she didn't take the plate. "Oh, come on. You have to eat something. Look at all this food," Malakai stated with a grand wave of his hand. "Look at all your favorites, and you aren't going to eat?" he continued with a knowing smile and a raised eyebrow.

"Kai, I can't. I'm still so worked up from the ceremony earlier. If I eat anything, I know it's going to turn my stomach," Diana answered, not even glancing in the direction of the food.

"Well then, it's a good thing pie isn't food," he said briskly, handing her the plate that already had a fork on it.

Diana stared down at the pie as if it was some otherworldly thing. She wasn't able to bring herself to do anything as mundane as eating. Not after today, not after everything.

She'd always known today would come and everything that was still to come after. None of it was a surprise to her, but she was surprised by how different she felt. It was as if the world itself had changed in the last few hours, and she was the only one who'd noticed.

Feeling the pressure of Malakai's intense stare, Diana finally ceded to his will. She picked up the fork and took a small bite. The flaky crust and the crispness of the apples were perfect. Diana closed her eyes and gave a little sigh of pleasure.

"I'll tell my mother you loved her pie, as usual," Malakai told her. Diana nodded, too busy methodically eating now to form words.

"Are you all right?" he asked her.

Malakai was a good head taller than her. His tall, muscular physique and charming smile made every girl in Terrene want to match with him. His dark brown eyes and sun-kissed tan from working outdoors made him particularly attractive. Diana had always tried hard not to think of her best friend that way. Unlike most, she saw his silly side, his selfish side, and even on occasion, his angry side. Diana knew everything about him, the good and bad.

Just now, when he looked down at her, the way his eyes were looking into hers, she felt the pit of her stomach lurch. The floor under her feet felt as if it had fallen away.

"I'm fine," she answered quickly. "It's just hot in here. Aren't you hot? Let's go outside."

All of her words came rushing out of her lips before she gave him the breath to answer. Diana set the empty plate down in a wash bin and turned to leave through the nearest door. Now that she'd said the word *outside*, it was all she could think of: the fresh air, the breeze, and the comfort of the trees.

Malakai nodded agreeably and took her arm as they left through the door. The hallway lined with people made Diana feel trapped. Smiling faces nodded their heads to her as she passed, wishing her well. A few held up cups and cheered to her health. It took a long time to get out of the hallway, away from the people, but Malakai's solid form was at her back, reassuring her.

They finally broke free of the crowd, swinging the door wide and entering the courtyard below. There were even more people out here than inside. A hail of cheers rang out through the air when they saw their new chief.

Diana forced herself to stand and wave. Malakai grabbed her elbow, smiling as charmingly as possible, ushered her through the sea of people, and kept walking until all the noise was behind them. Soon, the trees of the forest rose up out of the night to greet them.

"Thanks," Diana said, breathing hard as they came to the tree line. "I would've never gotten free by myself."

Malakai only nodded, his face going thoughtful and concerned. "Why don't we go sit by the stream?" he asked.

Diana nodded. They silently walked through the trees, arm in arm, to one of their favorite places. There was a beautiful shallow stream that ran near the castle. It was a place they'd found together, exploring and playing years ago. A little outcrop lay over the creek, where the grass was soft, and on warm days the shade was perfect, and the breeze was mild. It was a magical little spot, just for them.

Malakai spread out his brown cloak on the grass for them. They sat together under the starlight, watching the water glisten and listening to the sounds of the far away feast.

"If you don't tell me what's on your mind, I'm not going to stop pestering you until you get so irritated with me that you finally cave in and tell me," Malakai informed her, half laughing. "You know how annoying I can be."

Diana rolled her eyes. She knew only too well how irritating Malakai could be when he put his mind to it. "There's nothing wrong. Today was wonderful. Everything went exactly right. Everything was perfect, and now, I have nothing to worry about because it's all done."

"Well, I know it was a lot of work and stress for all of you. And I'm glad it's over. You looked beautiful today."

Diana's eyes were on the shimmering silver water down below, but at his words, she turned, looking into his suddenly serious face. All traces of his usually mischievous smile were gone.

She thought hard and couldn't recall a time where he'd ever called her beautiful. Malakai was always the one to tell her when she had ink smudged across her face or dirt in her hair. He'd told her once when she was ten that she looked pretty, but that was it.

Shaking off the feelings Diana saw in his face and felt in her heart, she turned the conversation to a more lighthearted topic. "Well, what are you doing tomorrow? Do you have to work?" she asked.

"Yes. I've got guard duty all day tomorrow. More than half the guards asked for the day off since they have family that traveled all this way for the ceremony. I don't mind. It'll keep me busy since I can't spend the day with you."

Diana looked away. Two sincere, serious comments like that from Malakai were too much for her to bear.

"I'll be busy all day tomorrow. In the morning, I'm meeting with my father to go over which chiefly duties he wants me to take over first, then after that..." Diana shrugged. "I've got so much to do. Everything I didn't get to today, and all the chores for tomorrow. I'll be lucky if I have a spare second anytime this week."

Malakai nudged her softly, and she smiled. He always did that to comfort her, his way of silently saying everything would be okay. "Aren't you done teaching now though? And shouldn't the majority of your other duties be taken over?"

"Well, yes," she conceded. "Alexander's the only replacement I've found so far. Everything else, I'm still looking for someone to help."

"I could help," Malakai said softly. "Name it."

A shiver ran down Diana's spine, and it wasn't from the breeze that suddenly shifted in their direction. She shook it off and gave a half-hearted laugh. "Oh, I doubt that you'll find anything fun in my new routine as chief. Everything I have to focus on now is jobs that you hate—finances and math, history, politics, gardening. The usual boring things you try to avoid at all costs."

"Well, that's true enough, but still, there must be something I can do to help you," he insisted.

Diana sighed. "Just stay my friend, okay? That's enough."

Malakai took her hand in his and surprised her by bringing it up to his lips. He laid a gentle kiss on it. The feeling of his lips on her skin sent a shiver of delight down to her toes.

"I wanted to talk to you about that," Malakai mentioned quietly.

The giddy sensation his lips had brought her plummeted down into her guts as hard as a stone. It was the moment she'd been dreading all day.

It wasn't the chiefing ceremony that terrified her, but what came after. Once Diana was crowned chief of Terrene, the next step in fulfilling her duties to her people was to get married and produce heirs.

Diana didn't know why the thought of settling down terrified her so, but it did, and worse still, children.

Diana loved teaching, but she felt she was too young and too inexperienced for anything remotely close to marriage and all that pertained to it, let alone having a child that she'd have to raise to be just like her.

It would be enough to churn anyone's stomach, she supposed; only other girls were so happy about the prospect. Diana wasn't sure if it was just inexperience at relationships that made her nervous or if it was who her potential suitors would be. Malakai was her best friend, but Diana had no idea how to go from best friend to boyfriend to husband in the short time she was allowed to have to make that decision.

"I don't want to talk about it," Diana said curtly, shaking her head as if to stop herself from thinking about it much more.

"But you know, tomorrow is officially the first day that you can receive proposals. I thought that—" Malakai didn't finish his sentence before Diana cut in with a sharp gesture.

"I said I don't want to talk about it. I know starting tomorrow, anyone in Terrene can ask me to marry them. I know it. And I don't even want to think about it," she insisted.

The thought of the proposals and the awkwardness that she'd feel about accepting and rejecting offers was horrible. She didn't know what to do. Her family had trained her to be chief, but ensuring that she had virtually no personal relationships beyond her few friends and family members made the task seem overwhelming.

"But I thought that—" Malakai began again.

"You thought wrong," Diana stated, getting angry now. Her hands were unconsciously clenching the fabric of her dress, wrinkling it. Before Malakai said anything else, before he could soothe her fears, she stood up abruptly and said, "I'm tired. I'm going to go. I'll see you tomorrow." Diana turned.

Malakai's eyes went wide with shock at her quick departure. "Wait."

She froze like a statue, hating how he made her feel so unsure of herself. Every girl in Castleton swooned over Malakai and made eyes at him. He could have anyone he wanted. But he was her best friend. Their parents were best friends. He was everyone's choice for her. But she didn't know what her own choice was.

She didn't know what she felt or how to describe it. She wanted to run and to put it off just a little longer until the God of Love told her if Malakai was the one she was supposed to be with. But if he wasn't, then what would she do? It was all so confusing.

Diana shook her head and didn't turn around, but she didn't need to. Malakai stood up, closing the space between them. His warm chest was searing her cold back as he pressed against her. She could feel the hard muscles under his shirt.

"I have something that I wanted to give you," he whispered against her skin.

"Please, no. Just..." but Diana's words trailed away as Malakai moved his arms around her.

She closed her eyes, giving way to the feeling of him. Then she felt it. Something cold and heavy as the gift settled onto her chest. She looked down, and nestled between her breasts was a white stone.

It was raw cut and beautiful, unlike any she'd ever seen before. Malakai had wrapped the stone with silver thread wire and tied it on a piece of white silk. The rock shone in the starlight, not white, but pink, blue, purple, and green as she moved it in her fingers.

"It's beautiful," she whispered, her eyes on the stone.

"Just like you are," he told her, his tone all sincerity. "I know you don't want to talk about marriage right now. So we won't. But you know what this means for you, for us. You have to know how I feel, how I've always felt about you. If you want to leave it, then I won't ask. But this is a promise that I'll never break."

Malakai's lips brushed against her temple, soft as a butterfly's wings, and then they were gone.

THE GORGON AND THE STRANGER

"Happy birthday," he said as he melted into the trees.

53

Author's Note

Thank you all so much for taking the time to read my short story.

The Bright One Series has been a work in progress for years, and I'm so excited to be able to share this teaser with the world.

Originally *The Gorgon and the Stranger* was meant to be a short story in a compilation that I was planning on printing after the main series concluded.

However, I loved the story so much that I changed it around just a tiny bit to make it work as an introduction to my writing and the world I created for my books.

I've always been an avid reader but never did I think that I'd be publishing my own books someday. It is truly amazing how life's twists and turns play out.

As it says in the book's conclusion, many characters that were hinted at in this short story will be seen again throughout the series. So, while it isn't essential as a reader to start with this book, it will be fun for those of you who enjoyed this enough to continue with my series, to make the connections as the series unfolds.

Through the Silent Forest is my first official book of the series, coming to publication soon.

If you enjoyed this short story, I'd love to hear about it and from you. You can contact me in various ways, either by a personal message through my website or a DM on Facebook or Instagram. I'd love to hear from you.

However, reviews make all the difference to an aspiring writer, so if you have time, I'd greatly appreciate a formal review on the respective retailor account or Goodreads if possible. If not, a simple post on your social media saying you enjoyed this will make my day. Be sure to tag me!

I look forward to hearing from you. Again, thank you so much for reading this. Feel free to follow if you're not already on my social media accounts for updates, cover art, and more as my publication progresses for my other books!

Love you all,

Ashley

Visit www.AshleyLCastillo.com for more details and links to all social media accounts.

Don't miss out!

Visit the website below and you can sign up to receive emails whenever Ashley L. Castillo publishes a new book. There's no charge and no obligation.

https://books2read.com/r/B-A-YLKO-AJIOB

Connecting independent readers to independent writers.

About the Author

About the Author

Ashley L. Castillo is a fantasy author with a passion for crafting unique worlds and fantastical adventures. As a lifelong fan of all things fantasy, Ashley loves to read books packed with mermaids, vampires, fairies and all kinds of mythical creatures. She hopes to entertain and inspire her readers by writing captivating novels with awe-inspiring settings and loveable characters. Ashley was born in Las Vegas, Nevada. When not writing, she enjoys traveling with her husband Josh and their three pets Bailey, Thomas and Kitten.

Read more at https://ashleylcastillo.wordpress.com.